PERSEPHONE
AND THE
POMEGRANATE SEEDS

AND
ATALANTA'S RACE

For Poppy

ORCHARD BOOKS

First published in Great Britain as part of "The Orchard
Book of Greek Myths" in 1992 by Orchard Books
This edition published in 2017 by The Watts Publishing Group

1 3 5 7 9 10 8 6 4 2

Text © Geraldine McCaughrean 1992
Illustrations © Tony Ross 1997

A CIP catalogue record for this book is available from the British Library.

ISBN 978 1 40835 129 1

Printed and bound in China by Imago

The paper and board used in this book are made from wood from responsible sources.

Orchard Books
An imprint of Hachette Children's Group
Part of The Watts Publishing Group Limited
Carmelite House, 50 Victoria Embankment, London EC4Y 0DZ

An Hachette UK Company
www.hachette.co.uk
www.hachettechildrens.co.uk

PERSEPHONE AND THE POMEGRANATE SEEDS

In those early days the weather was
always warm and sunny. The flowers
were always in bloom, the crops were
always ready for harvest. The goddess
Demeter tended the countryside like a
garden, planting seeds, watering the
green grass, encouraging the trees to
put on first blossom, then leaves,
then fruit.

And while Demeter worked, her little daughter Persephone used to play in the green woods of Sicily, picking violets until her apron was full. When mother and child walked home hand in hand at the end of another sunny day, talking and singing and laughing together, the evening primroses opened just to watch them pass by.

Pluto was not so lucky. Although he was a god, he did not live on the top of Mount Olympus in halls of cloud and sunlight, or on the earth among trees and fields. Pluto ruled over the Kingdom of the Dead, and lived under the earth in darkness and bitter cold. Not one ray of sunshine ever found its way down into those echoing caverns and tunnels.

But worse than either cold or dark was the loneliness.

Pluto tried to find a wife, but nobody wanted to give up the sunshine, the flowers, or the glittering sea to live in Pluto's dismal kingdom beneath the ground.

Sometimes Pluto would climb to the brim of the Underworld and peep out at the girls and women playing in the sun. The bright light hurt his eyes, but the sight of all those pretty women hurt even more.

One day he saw Persephone picking violets in her Sicilian wood.

"That's the one," murmured Pluto. "How beautiful she is! Oh yes, she's the wife for me."

But Pluto did not go to Demeter and ask to marry her daughter: he knew she would say no. Instead, he harnessed his black chariot and thundered out into the sunlight. Lashing his whip, he drove his horses on at full tilt. All Sicily shook at his coming, and his wheels felled trees to right and left as he raced through the woods. Holding the reins in his teeth, Pluto leaned out and snatched Persephone by her long hair. Her apron spilled all its violets.

"Who are you? What do you want with me? Oh let me go! Help me, somebody! Mother, help me!" she cried.

The trees bawled after Pluto, "Come back! Leave her alone!" Their green leaves flushed red with shouting, but Pluto took no notice as he raced back to his Underworld. He struck out with his whip. The earth split open. A bottomless ravine gaped, and his chariot sped downwards. Down into the dark, down into the cold, he carried Persephone.

"Don't cry," he told her. "I shall make you my queen. Be happy! I'll give you all the riches of the earth – gold and silver and gems! You have the love of a king! What more do you want?"

"I want to go home! I want my mother!" sobbed Persephone.

When they reached the River Styx, which divides the earth from the Kingdom of the Dead, she cried out, "River, help me! I am Persephone! Save me, please!"

The river heard her and knotted itself around the god's legs, almost tripping him. But Pluto kicked it aside

like a dog. In despair, Persephone slipped off her belt of flowers and threw it into the tumbling water. "Take that to my mother and tell her!" she pleaded. The river took her belt and hurried away. Then darkness closed in on all sides: Pluto had reached home with his captive wife.

Meanwhile, up on the earth, Demeter came looking for her daughter at the end of the day.

"Persephone darling! Time to go home!"

But there was no answer. Demeter called out and asked everyone she met, but it was hopeless.

Persephone had simply disappeared.

All Demeter's work was forgotten as she searched high and low for the child. Nothing mattered but to find Persephone. So the flowers wilted. The crops stopped growing. And as Demeter wept, the trees wept with her, shedding their leaves in brown and yellow tears.

After searching the world over, Demeter returned to Sicily and sat down in despair beside a river. As she gazed at the water, what should come spinning by on the current but a little cord of flowers.

"Persephone is in the Underworld," whispered the water. "I saw her! Pluto has stolen her away to be his queen."

Then Demeter ran all the way to Mount Olympus and rattled at the gates of heaven. "Zeus! Lord Zeus! Help me! Pluto has stolen away my daughter! Make him give her back!"

Zeus listened to poor Demeter. "You say your daughter was taken by force? Pluto shouldn't have done that. But there again—"

"Oh, Zeus!" she interrupted him. "If I don't get my daughter back, how shall I go on decking the earth with flowers and fruit? I only do it out of joy, and without Persephone there is no joy for me! Let the earth wither and die for all I care!"

Zeus shivered at the thought.

The little people on the earth would
quickly stop paying tribute to the gods
if their crops stopped growing and their
trees died.

"It's not up to me," he said gruffly.
"There are rules. If Persephone eats
anything while she is in the
Underworld, she cannot come back up
to earth. That's the rule."

"Then what are you waiting for?"
said Demeter. "Send your messenger
this instant!"

And though Zeus sent Hermes,
fastest flying of all the gods, Demeter
sped ahead of him that day, pulling on
his sleeve, begging him to hurry.

Meanwhile, below the earth, Pluto laid in front of Persephone a delicious feast. He knew (as she did not) that if she ate one mouthful she must stay with him for ever.

"I'm too miserable to eat," sobbed Persephone. "Let me go. Why don't you let me go? It's so dark and gloomy here!"

Pluto no longer thought his kingdom was dark or gloomy. Now that Persephone sat on a throne beside his, it seemed bright and cheerful. Hosts of ghosts came streaming through the darkness to gaze at his new bride. Pluto was very happy indeed.

"But you must eat, my dear. Just try a little something." He held up a dish of limes, an almond cake, a cup of broth, tempting her to eat.

"I'd rather die than eat your food," said Persephone, even though she was very, very hungry.

"Just a little taste." Pluto held up half a pomegranate – all red and juicy, smiling with seeds. He forced open her fingers and sprinkled twelve seeds into her palm.

Oh, and she was so very hungry!
For days she had sat and pined, hoping
her mother might find her. But her
mother did not come and did not come.
Persephone was too hungry to think.
She lifted the seeds to her lips ...

"Stop!"

Hermes, messenger of the gods, came skimming through the air in his winged sandals. "Noble Pluto! Zeus the Almighty commands you to let Persephone go ... Or am I too late?" He looked at the feast laid out in front of the two thrones.

"Yes, yes! You're too late!" crowed Pluto.

"No, no! What do you mean?" cried Persephone. Six little pomegranate seeds fell from the palm of her hand.

"Have you eaten any of those?" demanded Hermes. Persephone burst into tears.

"She has! She has!" cried Pluto triumphantly. "She's mine for ever!"

"Only a few!" pleaded Persephone. "What difference does it make?"

"Pluto, you're a rascal," said
Hermes. "You should have told her. I'm
sorry, Persephone. There's a rule, you
see. You have accepted Pluto's hospitality
– eaten his food. So now
you must stay here for ever."

"And hate you for ever, Pluto!"
cried Persephone, "because you
tricked me!"

When she said this, even Pluto turned a little pale. He loved Persephone and wanted her to love him in return. "I only stole you away because I was so lonely," he said, hanging his head.

Hermes felt sorry for them both. "Let Zeus decide!" he declared.

When Zeus heard what had
happened, he thought long and hard
before making his judgement. Finally,
he declared, "Because Persephone ate
six of the twelve pomegranate seeds, let
her live for six months of every year in
the Kingdom of the Dead. For the other
six months let her live with her mother,
on the earth ... And let no one argue
with the judgement of Zeus!"

And that is why, in the summertime,
the flowers bloom, the grass is
green and the trees wear blossom,
then leaves, then fruit. Demeter,
you see, is rushing happily here
and there, tending the
earth like a garden.
When she and her
daughter walk hand
in hand, talking and
singing and laughing,
the evening primroses
open just to see
them pass by.

But in the autumn, Persephone travels down to the Underworld, to keep her bargain with Pluto. First she learned to pity him. Then she learned to love him. And now the Underworld is much brighter and warmer during the six winter months. But up on the earth Demeter is missing her daughter. The trees flush red with calling Persephone's name, then drop their leaves. The flowers wither. The crops stop growing and the earth and the people of the earth wait for Persephone to return with the spring.

ATALANTA'S RACE

On the island of
Cyprus, in a lovely
garden tended by
Venus, the goddess of
love, there grew an
apple tree. It had
yellow branches
and yellow leaves,
but its apples were glittering gold.

Now, in the days when that tree was in fruit, there lived a beautiful girl called Atalanta. Men had only to see her to fall in love with her, but she had sworn never to marry. The young men pestered her to change her mind and grew tiresome. So she declared, "I will only marry the man who can race against me and win. But anyone who tries – and fails – must agree to die."

Despite the risk, many young men wanted to race Atalanta to win her hand. But she could run like the wind. The runners tried and the runners died, because they came in second.

A young man named Hippomenes had heard of Atalanta's races. He thought any boy must be stupid to throw his life away on a silly dare.

But when one day Atalanta streaked by
him, brown and fast as a darting
bird, he knew
at once that
he had to
race for her.

When Atalanta saw Hippomenes, she did not want him to challenge her. He was too young and handsome to die. She half wanted him to win ... but no! She had sworn never to marry.

A crowd gathered, impatient for another race, but Atalanta kept them waiting as she fretted about the result. And Hippomenes said his prayers.

"Oh, Venus!" prayed Hippomenes. "You plainly made me love this woman. So help me to win her!"

Venus heard him. She also thought Hippomenes too young and handsome to die. So she picked from the tree in her garden three golden apples and gave them to him. Now he was ready for the race.

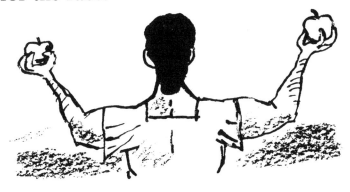

"Ready, steady, go!" cried the starter.

Away went Hippomenes, as fast as he had ever run. Away went Atalanta, quick as a blink. She soon took the lead.

So Hippomenes threw one golden
apple – beyond her, over her head. It
caught the light. Atalanta ran to where
it lay and picked it up. Hippomenes
sped ahead.

But Atalanta caught him up again
and passed him, hair blowing like a
flag. He ran faster than any of the
other suitors, but it was not fast
enough.

So Hippomenes threw another of the apples. Again Atalanta stopped to pick it up and again Hippomenes took the lead. But Atalanta was so much faster that she could stop, admire, pick up the shiny apples and still catch him up again.

Hippomenes ran faster than any man has ever run, but it was not fast enough. So he threw the third apple.

Would Atalanta be
fooled by the
trick a third
time? She saw –
she slowed down
– she glanced at
the two apples in
her hands ... And
she stopped for
the third.

The crowd cheered as Hippomenes dashed past her, lungs bursting, and threw himself over the winning line. He had won his bride!

And for a champion runner who has just lost a race for the first time, Atalanta looked extremely happy.